Read with Me
STORIES

By Terry Dinning
Illustrated by Angela Kincaid

Brimax · Newmarket · England

4

Freddy Fox

"Do you want to go out to play with your friends, Freddy?" asks Freddy's mother.

"I do not want to go out because it is raining," says Freddy.

"Why not?" says Mrs Fox. She is sewing and wants some peace and quiet.

"I do not want to get my tail wet," says Freddy. He is very proud of his beautiful, red tail.

Outside Freddy sees his friend Desmond Duck. Desmond is splashing in the stream.

"Come and play!" he calls.

"I do not want to get my tail wet," calls Freddy.

"If you put your boots on and take an umbrella, you will not get wet," says Mrs Fox.

Freddy goes upstairs to look for his boots and his umbrella.
He looks under the bed. But they are not there. He looks in his wardrobe. But they are not there either.
Freddy hears his mother calling him. "Your boots and your umbrella are down here."
Freddy runs downstairs and is soon ready to go out to play.

Wilbur Weasel comes to play. He shakes his wet fur all over Freddy.
"Look out!" shouts Freddy.
"Rain is horrible. What can we do?"
"Lots of things," says Desmond.
"First we can play a splashing game. We must find a big puddle, then jump in it as hard as we can. The biggest splash wins!"

Everyone chooses a big puddle and jumps in it as hard as they can. Splash! Desmond makes a big splash. Splash! Wilbur makes a big splash. SPLASH! Freddy makes the biggest splash of all. "This is fun," says Freddy.

"Excuse me," says a voice from high in the branches of a tree. "I don't think it is fun. You've made my feathers very wet."

Olly Owl flutters his wet wings. "Please stop that at once!" he hoots.

They all scamper away. Freddy's tail is wet at the tip, but he does not notice.

"What shall we do now?" asks Freddy.

"I know," says Wilbur. "We can make some paper boats and sail them along the stream."

The paper boats float along the water.

"We can have a race with the boats," cries Desmond. "Let's go!" The three friends cheer their little boats along the stream. Freddy drops half his tail in the water, but he does not notice - his boat is winning the race! Desmond swims beside the boats. "Look at me," he calls. "I am pretending to be a yellow boat."

"I wish we could all pretend to be boats," says Freddy. Then he has an idea. He takes his umbrella, turns it upside-down and sets it on the water. It floats just like a boat. He jumps into the umbrella. "I am the captain of this boat," he says. Wilbur jumps in beside him. Freddy's tail falls over the side and gets very wet, but he does not notice. He is too busy sailing his umbrella boat.

Then Desmond says, "Time to go home. Come on, everyone." Desmond begins to swim back up the stream. He looks over his shoulder, but Freddy and Wilbur are not behind him. They cannot make the umbrella boat turn around. The stream is carrying them further and further away!

"Help us!" they cry.

Then Mrs Duck swims along. She is looking for Desmond. She sees the umbrella with Freddy and Wilbur in it and quickly swims after it. She pulls it safely to the bank.

"Thank you," gasps Freddy.

He is soaking wet, but he does not notice - he is too busy catching his breath!

25

Everyone goes back to Freddy's house to dry in front of the fire. Soon, Freddy, Desmond and Wilbur are sitting in front of the fire drinking hot milk and eating cookies. Suddenly Freddy remembers his tail.

"My poor tail," says Freddy.

"You must be very careful when you play near water," scolds Mrs Fox. Mrs Duck has an idea. "I will teach Freddy and Wilbur to swim like ducks," she says. "Then they can play safely in the stream."
"Now, Freddy," says Mrs Fox, "I have a surprise for you. Close your eyes." Freddy closes his eyes.

"Now you can look," says Mrs Fox.
She shows Freddy what she has
been sewing. It is a bright yellow
raincoat!
"You will look just like me," says
Desmond.
"I will swim like a duck and look
like a duck," laughs Freddy.

Say these words again.

friends   puddle
raining   feathers
beautiful   scamper
stream   sail
winning   yellow
stairs   shoulder
splashing   remembers

What can you see?

tail

umbrella

boots

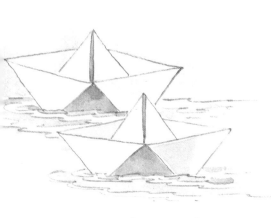

paper boats

raincoat

Benjamin Rabbit

Benjamin Rabbit is very busy. He
and his friends are going to the
beach for a picnic, and he is
helping to fill the baskets.
Mr Rabbit is making lots of
sandwiches and Mrs Rabbit is
icing the cake. There are cookies,
pies and lemonade. The kitchen
is full as everyone helps.

37

Suddenly they hear a "Toot-toot!" outside. It is Mr Bear, the train driver. He is taking everyone to the beach in his little stream train. "Come along!" he calls. Benjamin's friends are already on the train. Freddy Fox, Billy Bear, Wilbur Weasel, Daisy Dormouse and Desmond Duck are all waiting.

"Wait for me!" cries Benjamin. He runs up with the bulging basket. Mr Bear helps him and the basket onto the train. "Off we go," says Mr Bear. The little train puffs along in the sunshine. Benjamin is sure that this is going to be a special day. The train soon arrives at the beach. "Here we are," says Mr Bear. "Everybody out!"

The sky is blue and the sea is calm. The sand is golden and warm. Benjamin jumps out of the train and pulls off his shoes and his socks. The sand is soft between his toes. "I will race you down to the sea," he calls to his friends, and off they go. Freddy Fox is the winner.

43

The waves rush up the sand to meet them and Benjamin's toes get wet. "The sea is chasing me," he laughs. They all splash about happily in the water.

45

Mr Bear is setting out the picnic.
"Time for lunch," he calls. Everyone
is very hungry. They eat the
sandwiches, cake and cookies.
"More lemonade, please," says
Benjamin.
"Pass the cookies, please," says
Wilbur.
They are all too full to run around
anymore!
"What shall we do now?" says
Freddy.

"Now we can build a sandcastle," says Benjamin. They decide to make the biggest sandcastle anyone has ever seen.

"We can put all these shells and stones on the sandcastle," says Freddy. They all set to work. The sandcastle grows and grows.

49

Benjamin goes for a walk along the beach with Daisy and Desmond. They find a sparkling rock pool. In the pool they find a starfish, a jellyfish and long ribbons of seaweed. Benjamin finds lots of shells and smooth, shiny stones. He takes them back to show the others.

51

Then Benjamin hears a tiny voice calling. It is coming from the sea. "Hello," says the voice.

He goes to see who is there. Swimming about in the waves he see a little mermaid! Her eyes are as blue as the sea. Her hair is as golden as the sand. She has a fish's tail instead of legs.

"Hello," says Benjamin.

"Can you help me please?" says the little mermaid. "I have lost the big, blue stone from my new necklace. The sea has taken it and it must be on the beach. Can you find it for me?"

"We will all look for it," says Benjamin. He tells his friends about the little mermaid's lost stone and everyone starts to search for it.

They all find something. Daisy finds a starfish. Billy finds a shell. Wilbur finds a crab. Freddy finds some seaweed. Desmond finds a pebble. But no one can find the mermaid's lost stone.

"Oh dear," says Benjamin. "We have looked everywhere. Where can it be?"

Then he sees something shining on the top of the sandcastle.

"Here is your stone," cries Benjamin. It was on top of the sandcastle the whole time.
The little mermaid is very happy to have her blue stone back.
"Thank you," she says. Now I will give you something." She gives Benjamin a great big sea shell.

59

"Put it up to your ear," she says.
"I can hear the sea," says
Benjamin in surprise.
"Yes," smiles the mermaid. "Now
you will always be able to hear
the sea, wherever you are."
On the way home, Benjamin
listens to the sea shell. He will
never forget his special day at
the beach.

61

Say these words again.

picnic	ribbons
sandwiches	around
kitchen	voice
sunshine	instead
golden	blue
special	surprise
sparkling	beach

What can you see?

train

basket

sandcastle

mermaid

blue stone

Gilda the Witch

It is morning in the forest. Gilda the witch turns over in bed. "Time for another little snooze," she says sleepily.

Gilda takes care of the forest with her magic spells. Her cottage is full of magical things. She has a broomstick, a cauldron, a crystal ball and shelves full of books. She also has a cat called Timothy.

Timothy leaps up onto Gilda's bed and licks the end of her nose. "What is the matter Timothy?" mumbles Gilda. "Why are you waking me up?" She sits up in bed, and the tip of her witches' hat falls down over one eye. "What is that noise?" she wonders. She hears a strange noise outside.

Gilda leaps out of bed. Through the window she can see Katie and Bobby Rabbit scampering away in the distance. The sky is blue, the grass is green and the daisies are white and yellow. "How lovely!" sighs Gilda. "Today my spells will sweeten the bees' honey and make the roses smell like perfume."

Gilda is stirring her cauldron when there is a knock at the door. It is Sally Squirrel. "Have you seen what has happened to the forest?" she squeaks. Gilda hurries outside. The trees are as tall as ever. The flowers smell as sweet as ever. Then Gilda sees what is wrong. The sky is not blue. It is green! The grass is not green. It is blue!

"One minute the sky was blue, and now it is green," says Sally. "You must cast a spell to make everything right again."

"I need my magic spell book," says Gilda. She hunts along the bookshelves. She hunts under the table. She hunts among the cushions. "Where did I put that spell book?"

Timothy jumps onto the window-sill. He gives a loud meeow. "Are you trying to tell me something?" asks Gilda. Suddenly she remembers what happened that morning, when she heard someone laughing outside the window. Gilda stares at the blue grass and the violet daisies. There are tiny footprints on the grass. "Those look like rabbits' footprints!" she says to herself.

"I know what has happened,"
Gilda tells Sally. "Someone has
taken my spell book and I think I
know who. Have you seen Bobby
and Katie Rabbit this morning?"
"No," says Sally.
"When we find Bobby and Katie,
I think we will find the spell book,"
says Gilda. "Then we can put
everything right again. Come
and help me look."

Gilda, Sally and Timothy set out on the trail of the missing spell book. Gilda flies along on her broomstick. Sally jumps from tree to tree. Timothy marches along with his whiskers in the air. They ask everyone they meet if they have seen Bobby and Katie.

"No," says Emma Duckling.

"No," says Hetty Hare.

"No," says Rosie Rabbit.

"No," says George Bear who is busy in his garden. "I hope you find your book soon. I cannot tell my plums from my peaches until everything is put right again."
Then Timothy begins to sniff at the bushes. He can hear something. He meeows again. Gilda can hear something too. It sounds just like two little rabbits crying.

"Is that you, Katie and Bobby?" calls Gilda. Katie and Bobby creep out from the bushes. Bobby is carrying Gilda's spell book. "You naughty little rabbits," scolds Gilda. "It was very wrong to take my book without asking." "We are sorry," sniffs Katie. "We only wanted to borrow the book, but we did not want to wake you."

"We wanted to make some magic spells," says Bobby. "We must have mixed them up, because when we said the magic words the sky turned green. And look!" Katie and Bobby turn around. Their tiny tails are not white, but blue! "Never mind, you can help stir the cauldron while I say the spell that will change everything back to normal again," says Gilda.

Everyone goes home to Gilda's cottage. They wait while she finds all the magic things she needs. She needs early morning dew, some moonlight from a silver bottle, some cobwebs, and two hairs from a rabbit's tail.

"It does not matter if they are blue," she says. Then she reads out the magic spell from her book. "Abracadabra!" she cries.

They rush to the window. Gilda's spell has worked! The sky is blue. The grass is green. "Well done," says Sally. "You are a good witch, Gilda." But Katie and Bobby still have their blue tails.

"They will be white again in a few days," Gilda says to them. "That will teach you not to meddle with magic!"

Say these words again.

forest	right
snooze	cushions
magic	laughing
cottage	whiskers
window	suddenly
distance	borrow
sweeten	meddle

What can you see?

broomstick

cauldron

spell book

cat

crystal ball